GHOST DETECTORS

Draw!

BOOK 5

BY
DOTTI ENDERLE

ILLUSTRATED BY
HOWARD MCWILLIAM

magic
wagon

visit us at www.abdopublishing.com

A special thanks to Melissa Markham—DE
With thanks for my ever-supportive wife Rebecca—HM

Published by Magic Wagon, a division of the ABDO Group,
8000 West 78th Street, Edina, Minnesota 55439. Copyright
© 2010 by Abdo Consulting Group, Inc. International copyrights
reserved in all countries. All rights reserved. No part of this
book may be reproduced in any form without written permission
from the publisher.

Calico Chapter Books™ is a trademark and logo of Magic Wagon.

Printed in the United States.

Text by Dotti Enderle
Illustrations by Howard McWilliam
Edited by Stephanie Hedlund and Rochelle Baltzer
Cover and interior design by Jaime Martens

Library of Congress Cataloging-in-Publication Data
Enderle, Dotti, 1954-
    Draw! / by Dotti Enderle ; illustrated by Howard McWilliam.
       p. cm. -- (Ghost Detectors ; bk. 5)
    Summary: When forced on a camp-out with their fathers, ten-
year-olds Malcolm and Dandy seek the smelly ghost of notorious
outlaw Wild Willy Wallace, who is believed to haunt his old
hideout at Lake Itchyburr.
    ISBN 978-1-60270-694-1
    [1. Ghosts--Fiction. 2. Haunted places--Fiction. 3. Camping--
Fiction. 4. Fathers and sons--Fiction. 5. Humorous stories.] I.
McWilliam, Howard, 1977- ill. II. Title.
    PZ7.E69645Drc 2009
    [Fic]--dc22
                                    2008055326

Contents

No Give

"**D**o we have to go?" Malcolm asked his dad as they sat at the dinner table.

"Camping is fun, Malcolm. And it's good for you," Dad answered from behind his newspaper.

Good for you? Malcolm would rather eat worms than go camping. Malcolm's father, along with Dandy's dad, had planned a crisp weekend at Lake

Itchyburr. The dads claimed it'd be a chance to get back to nature, but Malcolm figured it was really just a chance for the grown-ups to try to outfish each other.

Malcolm's sister, Cocoa, bit down on a carrot, which Malcolm couldn't help but notice was the same color as her lip gloss. "I'm glad I don't have to go. I hate camping," she said.

"That's baloney," Malcolm argued. "You camp out every day . . . in the bathroom!"

Cocoa sneered at him as she loudly chomped her food.

Grandma Eunice sat staring at her plate. *Zzzzzzzzzz.*

"Grandma!" Malcolm nudged her. "You're sleeping with your eyes open again."

Grandma shook her head, clearing the cobwebs. "I don't like carrots. I like beans."

"We don't have beans," Mom said.

Malcolm tried another attempt to get out of the trip. "I just don't think it's healthy to go camping in the fall. It's chilly at night. We could catch a cold."

Dad folded the newspaper and set it down. He looked over at Malcolm, then shook his head. "Son, you look like paste."

Here we go again! Malcolm thought. Dad's continual song and dance about the health factors of getting outdoors.

"This camping trip is a chance to get you out of that basement. I mean, you practically live down there."

Cocoa puckered her lips in a hideous smirk. "Correction, Dad. It's not a

basement, it's his dungeon." She moved in so close Malcolm could smell the pork chops mingling with her dragon breath.

"Correction, Coconut. It's a lab," Malcolm said. "If it were a dungeon we'd have you chained in it."

"I'd rather have beans," Grandma Eunice complained.

"My point is," Dad continued, ignoring them, "you don't get out enough. You never participate in any sports. You should play soccer, go biking, go skateboarding . . . anything."

"Skateboarding?" Malcolm said. "Can I build the skateboard myself?"

Mom and Dad gave each other a panicked look. "No!"

Would they ever forgive him for the time he applied blasters to the backs of his

Rollerblades? After all, it had hurt him more than the fence.

Malcolm went back to eating.

Grandma Eunice picked up her fork. "Beans, beans, the musical fruit . . . "

"Grandma!" Mom quickly interrupted. Then she looked at Malcolm with concern. "Dad is right, sweetheart. You're turning into a mole."

"A pasty mole," Cocoa added.

"Yeah, like that hairy one on your face," Malcolm said, poking her chin with a dot of potatoes.

"Malcolm!" Cocoa wiped at it with her fist.

Mom and Dad were now giving him the laser eyes. "Seriously, Malcolm," Dad said. "This is my chance to get you out of

that basement. I know you'll enjoy it. There's fishing and hiking. And maybe you and Daniel could throw a Frisbee or something."

"Fine," Malcolm said under his breath. Maybe he could turn the Frisbee into a flying saucer and give his ghost dog, Spooky, a ride.

"Just be packed and ready," Dad went on. "We're leaving as soon as school is out tomorrow.

Malcolm scarfed down his food, wanting to get down to his lab. Grandma Eunice nudged him under the table. "Don't forget the other fun part of camping," she whispered.

Malcolm looked at her questioningly. "What?" he whispered back.

"Ghost stories."

A New Invention

"I don't get it," Dandy said, slurring his words through a wad of purple bubble gum. "Shouldn't you be packing?"

Dandy had come over right after dinner to get a checklist from Malcolm on what they should take. He flipped on Malcolm's Ecto-Handheld-Automatic-Heat-Sensitive-Laser-Enhanced Specter Detector.

Yip! Yip!

"Hey, Spooky!" Dandy said to Malcolm's ghostly dog, who had followed them home from a ghost-hunting adventure the past summer.

"Dad wants me to be more active. He wants us to throw a Frisbee."

Dandy's eyes became teeny slits. He clearly didn't understand. "We're going to throw a Frisbee?"

"Wrong," Malcolm said. "We're going to invent something that'll throw it for us."

Dandy nodded and smacked his gum. It sounded like someone jogging through mud.

Malcolm dug into his box of doodads. It was mostly old appliances, utensils, and his mom's hand vac. He'd been saving them to make a device to capture ghosts. "This should do it," he said, pulling up an old toaster.

"Won't the Frisbee melt in there?" Dandy asked.

"No, Dandy. I've already taken out the heating coils." *Why can't Dandy imagine things properly?* Malcolm scratched his head, trying to figure out how to get the toaster to pop up without electricity.

Dandy stopped chewing. "Uh, Malcolm? I don't think a Frisbee will fit in there."

Malcolm sighed. "We don't have to use a real Frisbee—just something Frisbee-like. Let me think."

"A plate?" Dandy suggested.

"Nope. That'd be too big."

"A saucer?"

Malcolm looked up. "Wouldn't that break on impact?"

"Not if I catch it."

"What if you don't?"

Dandy shrugged and popped a huge bubble. "A plastic saucer?"

"You're kinda on the right track," Malcolm said. "Think thinner."

"A lid? A coaster? A slice of bologna?"

"Bologna?"

"Sorry," Dandy said. "I'm hungry." He popped another whopper of a bubble.

Malcolm's brain was working in overdrive. He knew there had to be something that would fit in the toaster. Something small and round like a flying saucer. His mind was seeing circles.

"I've got it!" he yelled, causing Dandy to pop a bubble too soon. He looked at Malcolm through a mask of purple gum.

Yip! Yip! Spooky jumped up, trying to lick the gum off Dandy's face.

Malcolm didn't bother explaining. He ran and opened another box he'd tucked away on the shelf. "How about these?" He held up some blank CDs.

Dandy picked strands of gum off his chin since Spooky's tongue couldn't do the job.

Malcolm tested the CDs. Perfect fit.

"So we're going to play Frisbee with those?" Dandy asked.

"Yeah, I think so," Malcolm replied, checking the toaster's springs to see if he could make them pop manually.

Dandy looked down at his hands, then at Malcolm. "And I'm supposed to catch them?"

"Sure," Malcolm said, still tinkering.

15

Dandy looked back at his hands. "Malcolm?"

"What?"

"Won't a CD slice my fingers off?" He held up his fingers, which were laced with purple gum curls.

"Dandy, do I have to think of everything? It's simple. You use gloves."

Dandy grinned. "Okay."

"Now," Malcolm said, "I need something to attach to this handle. Something like a rubber band."

Dandy dug in his pocket and pulled out two pennies, a dead snail, and a rubber band. "Here you go." The rubber band was thin and flimsy.

"It'll break too easy. I need something sturdy, like a bungee cord."

Dandy scratched his head, leaving sticky purple tracks on his hair.

"Come with me," Malcolm said, tucking the toaster under his arm. "I know the perfect thing."

"Where are we going?"

Malcolm gave Dandy a sly grin. "To the bathroom. That's where Cocoa leaves all her elastic ponytail holders."

"Do you think they'll work?" Dandy asked.

"If they can hold back that mop on Cocoa's head, they have to be strong!"

Dandy switched off the ghost detector, sending Spooky back to his ghostly realms. "So what else should I pack?" he asked as they climbed the basement stairs.

"Gloves," Malcolm said.

The Great Outdoors

After the two-hour car ride to Lake Itchyburr, Malcolm and Dandy were ready to stretch their legs. While their dads rode comfortably up front, the boys were crammed into the backseat.

They were poked by fishing poles and smushed by sleeping bags. Dandy spent a good ten minutes trying to untangle his foot from a dipping net. When they rolled into the campground, the boys both let out sighs of relief.

"Smell that fresh air!" Malcolm's dad said, taking a deep breath.

Malcolm inhaled what seemed to be a mixture of mold, car exhaust, and swamp scum. "Ew . . . it doesn't smell so great to me."

Dandy opened his car door and fell out in an avalanche of camping gear. "Hey! Can someone help me out here?"

His dad reached over and lifted him up. "Thanks for unloading the car, son."

"No problem, Dad," Dandy said, rubbing the knot on his head where the minnow bucket had clobbered him.

Malcolm's father looked at his watch. "Let's get those tents pitched before dark."

"Where?" Dandy asked.

Malcolm's dad pointed to a spot by a clump of trees. "That area looks perfect."

Dandy's mouth dropped into an O. "I don't think we can throw them that far."

The dads both laughed.

"*Pitching a tent* means setting it up," Malcolm said.

"That's good," Dandy said. "'Cause I bruised my throwing arm when I fell out of the Jeep."

The dads each had a large dome tent for themselves, while Malcolm and Dandy set up a small pup tent to share. It was so small they could barely cram their sleeping bags inside.

"If you get too cramped, you can share one of our tents," Malcolm's dad offered.

"We'll be fine," Malcolm assured him.

"Well then, let's get the campfire going so we can cook up some grub."

Dandy's eyes lit up. "Yay! I'm hungry."

Malcolm's dad pointed to a Cypress tree. "You boys head over there to find some thin branches."

"For kindling?" Malcolm asked.

"For forks," Dad said. "We can use them to roast hot dogs and toast marshmallows."

Dandy's eyes grew even bigger. "Yay! I like marshmallows."

Malcolm and Dandy found some low forked branches. They skewered their hot dogs and held them over the fire to cook.

The sun was a red ball, dipping in the west. The nighttime noises of the woods began to sing. Most people would find the crickets, frogs, and crackle of a fire peaceful, but Malcolm kept imagining a large, furry, apelike creature tearing through the trees.

"You think Bigfoot lives out here?" he asked.

The dads laughed. "I don't think so, son," Malcolm's dad replied.

Dandy also looked a little rattled. "What about snakes?"

"I think you should be more worried about wearing your bug spray," his dad answered.

Dandy turned his wiener over and it slipped off into the fire. He stabbed it a couple of times before bringing it back. Then he blew the ashes off the side that was now black and crusty.

Malcolm flipped his hot dog too. The juices were dripping, causing the fire to hiss. He looked around at the darkened campground. "Anyone know any ghost stories?"

Dandy raised his hand. "And mine are true, too!"

Malcolm grabbed Dandy's arm, lowering his hand. "I know all those."

Dandy's dad rolled his stick with his palms, twirling his hot dog like a propeller. "Don't know about ghost stories," he said, "but Lake Itchyburr has a famous ghost legend."

Malcolm and Dandy both perked up. "A ghost legend?" Malcolm asked.

Mr. Dee nodded. "Lake Itchyburr was the hideout of the infamous outlaw Wild Willy Wallace."

"An outlaw?" Malcolm asked.

"Yep. And it's said that his ghost roams these very woods."

The Legend of
Wild Willy Wallace

Mr. Dee stopped twirling his hot dog stick and sat staring at it. His eyes looked distant. "Wild Willy Wallace," he began, "was the most ornery varmint to step foot in these parts. They say his heart was pure black. He robbed banks and trains and sometimes people. It's even said that that no-good outlaw snatched a piece of candy right out of a toddler's hand. Like I said, a heart of black."

He paused a moment, tending to his hot dog. "So what happened?" Dandy asked. Malcolm was also eager to hear the tale.

"Like all outlaws, Wild Willy needed a place to hide. Lake Itchyburr seemed like the perfect spot. Not only did he have the cloak of all the thick trees, but there are hidden caverns in these hills as well. Wild Willy chose one for his hideout.

"Now keep in mind, he didn't work alone. He had a gang of shady characters that pulled off those robberies with him. All of them tied bandanas over their mouths and noses. Only their beady dark eyes peeked out. They terrorized the countryside, whooping and hollering and taking whatever they could get."

Malcolm had gotten so caught up in the story, he'd forgotten about his hot dog. He quickly turned it over. The side left

unattended was now charred as black as the wiener Dandy had dropped into the fire. Malcolm didn't care. He just listened.

"After robbing the Central Freight Express," Mr. Dee went on, "Willy and his gang holed up here. They hid those bags of gold and jewelry in one of the caves."

Dandy's face lit up in the firelight. "Is that money and gold still hidden out here?"

"I'm not sure, son," his dad answered. "Some say it is. But this legend isn't about lost gold. It's about Wild Willy himself. You see, Willy was a selfish devil. Oh sure, in the beginning he split the stolen goods evenly with his gang. They divided it fair and square.

"But Wild Willy started thinking maybe he should get more. After all, he was the brains of the operation. The other boys

just went along with whatever Wild Willy said.

"So after a few bank robberies, Willy told them the plan. He intended to keep half for himself and let them split the rest. When they argued, Willy told them it was his face on the wanted posters. The $25,000 reward was for him, not for any of them."

"But I thought they wore those bandanas over their faces," Dandy interrupted.

"Shhhh, Dandy!" Malcolm said. "Let him finish."

"They did wear bandanas," Mr. Dee continued. "But plenty of people are recognized by their eyes. The group knew they could be recognized too, and they couldn't chance it. That gang flat-out told Wild Willy that the gold would be split

evenly or they wanted out. Well, Willy knew he couldn't do it alone, so he agreed. But he had a plan.

"The next train robbery happened to be the biggest payroll shipment this side of the river. After it was over, Willy stored the money in one of the Lake Itchyburr caverns as usual.

"That night, when the rest of his gang was sleeping, Willy dragged that money out and strapped it to his saddle. He'd planned to take it all and ride off into the night. But when he came back with the last sack, all four gang members stood blocking the way. 'Where you going?' they asked.

"Willy knew he was stuck. He tried to think up an excuse. But it turns out, he wasn't as smart as he thought he was. 'I think this cave is too much in the open,'

Willy said. 'I was just moving the money to safer place.'

"Well, those boys weren't buying that story at all. 'We think you're planning on hightailing it out of here, leaving us high and dry,' they told him. They moved in closer. He knew he was outnumbered, but he reached for his gun. His gang drew first. And when Wild Willy fell, he fell hard . . . right into a polecat nest."

"A polecat nest?" Malcolm asked.

"Yep," Mr. Dee said. "A big nest of skunks."

"Phew!" Dandy said, lifting his blackened wiener from the fire.

"And it's said," Mr. Dee continued, "that Wild Willy's ghost still haunts these parts."

Malcolm rescued his own hot dog from the campfire. "Really?" he asked.

Mr. Dee nodded. "And you always know when he's around because you can smell him coming."

"That's awesome," Malcolm said. "Another stinky ghost!"

Malcolm's dad patted his son's back. "I think we have enough to worry about with the skunks smelling things up around here. I hope we don't encounter a smelly ghost, too."

But Malcolm didn't agree at all. After all, he took his job as a ghost hunter very seriously. He'd already zapped an intruder, helped his teacher's husband, and given an actress her chance to shine. He was glad he'd brought his specter detector on the trip so he could hunt an outlaw!

Sneaking Out

After stuffing themselves with burnt hot dogs and roasted marshmallows, the boys crawled into their small tent. They slipped into their sleeping bags, leaving on the small lantern.

The woods were quiet. Not many night creatures stirred. But there was one mosquito that kept buzzing around Dandy. He swatted and swatted, missing it every time.

"Zip yourself up so it can't reach you," Malcolm said.

Dandy did. He looked like a mummy in his sleeping bag, with only his eyes peeping out.

"Don't get too comfortable," Malcolm told him.

"Wuh wee goon ou?" Dandy mumbled.

"What?"

Dandy repeated, "Wuh wee goon ou?"

Malcolm unzipped Dandy's sleeping bag down to his chin. "What?"

The mosquito landed on Dandy's nose. "I said, what are we gonna do?" He swatted hard at the mosquito. It flew off, causing Dandy to pop himself in the nose. "Ouch!"

"We're going to wait for snoring," Malcolm said.

Dandy's eyes circled, keeping watch on that pesky mosquito. "Snoring?"

"Yeah. Both our dads snore like angry bears. Once we hear them, then we'll know it's safe."

Dandy tried grabbing at the mosquito this time. "Safe for what?"

"Safe to go looking for Wild Willy Wallace."

Dandy sat straight up. "We're not going out there tonight, are we?"

Malcolm pulled out his specter detector. "Why not?"

"This isn't just any ghost," Dandy said, snatching at the pesky bug again. "It's a notorious outlaw!"

Malcolm pulled out his ghost zapper. "So?"

Dandy's face had turned the color of straw. Malcolm wasn't sure if it was from fright or the lantern glow.

"I think we should just let his legend live on," Dandy said.

"Come on, Dandy! This is what we do. We're ghost hunters, remember?"

Dandy lay back down. "Oh . . . okay."

It didn't take long before they heard snoring from both of their dads' tents.

"They do sound like angry bears," Dandy said.

Quietly slipping out, Malcolm held the lantern low in order to see the path.

Dandy took tiny, careful steps. "This doesn't feel very safe."

"We're not going far," Malcolm assured him. He was about to flip on his ghost

detector when something caused him to freeze. He looked at Dandy. "Smell that?"

Dandy took a huge whiff. "Ew! It smells like a skunk!" Then his eyes grew big. "Malcolm, do you think it's him?"

Malcolm put a finger to his lips. "Shhhhh!" He tiptoed a little closer, pulling out his ghost zapper. The smell grew stronger. "He's definitely here," he whispered.

Dandy followed, looking like he might turn and run at any moment.

Malcolm held the ghost zapper at the ready. He wouldn't waste a moment pulling the trigger. The smell grew stronger.

"Over there," Dandy said, pointing to a small hiking trail just off the path. They made their way over. That's when they saw it, glowing white.

Dandy stood so close that Malcolm could feel him breathing on his neck. "Do you see it?" Malcolm asked.

Dandy nodded, too scared to speak. The white glow floated closer, and the smell grew stronger. "Zap it now!" Dandy whispered.

But Malcolm waited. It moved in closer . . . and closer. "It's too small to be Wild Willy Wallace," Malcolm said.

That's when it waddled right in front of them.

"Skunk!" Dandy yelled. Both boys turned and hightailed it back to their tent. They ducked in, falling back onto their sleeping bags.

"Maybe we should go ghost hunting tomorrow," Malcolm said.

The Super Toss

"Rise and shine!" Malcolm's dad said, poking his head into the small tent.

"Ugh," Malcolm said, rolling onto his side.

"Up and at 'em," his dad egged.

Malcolm opened one bleary eye. He could see the large lump that was Dandy, zipped all the way into his sleeping bag. Small snores that sounded like a hissing cockroach rose up from within. *Sssssssss* . . .

Malcolm closed his sleepy eye.

"Come on, snoozy," Dad said. "We're going fishing."

"Ugh," Malcolm repeated. "Dad, I'm not going fishing."

"Sure you are, silly. Why do you think we came out here to begin with?"

"To get me out of the basement."

"Right," Dad agreed. "And to go fishing."

"No, you and Mr. Dee planned this trip to fish. Dandy and I just came along."

"Son, let's not argue. Just get up."

Malcolm opened both eyes this time. Dandy hadn't moved a smidge.

Sssssssss . . .

"You and Mr. Dee go ahead. Dandy and I are going to throw the Frisbee."

His dad made a huffing noise. It was the same noise he made while waiting for Grandma Eunice to get out of the bathroom. "You can't throw the Frisbee right now, silly. It's still dark."

"Dark?" Malcolm peeked out of the tent. The sky was full of twinkling stars. "What time is it?"

His dad tilted his wrist then clicked the light display on his watch. "About four thirty."

"Four thirty!" Four thirty still seemed like the middle of the night to Malcolm. "Just go without us. Dandy and I have plans when we wake up."

"What type of plans?"

Malcolm fell back onto his sleeping bag. "Throwing the Frisbee. Right, Dandy?"

Sssssssss . . .

"Fine," Dad said. "We'll be back in a few hours."

Malcolm closed his eyes and was soon back in dreamland.

After a breakfast of Pop-Tarts and orange juice, the boys headed out. The reddish sun was rising above the trees.

"Where are we going?" Dandy asked, strolling beside Malcolm.

"We need to be in an open area to try out the Super Toss."

Dandy cocked his head. "The Super Toss?"

"Yeah," Malcolm said. "That's what I'm calling the Frisbee thrower." He had the geared-up toaster under his arm.

"Aren't we going to look for Wild Willy Wallace?" Dandy asked.

"Yeah. But I promised my dad."

"You promised him you'd throw a Frisbee, not launch one out of a toaster."

"It's a Super Toss, not a toaster."

"Whatever," Dandy said.

"This looks like a good place." Malcolm did a full turn. The clearing was large, with a couple of trail entrances. Just beyond was heavy brush and rock that went on and on toward the lake.

"Go stand over there." He pointed to a spot on the other side, just near the tall weeds and scrappy bushes.

Dandy headed over while Malcolm prepared the Super Toss.

"Ready?" Malcolm called.

"Not yet," Dandy said. He reached into his back pocket and pulled out some heavy gloves.

Malcolm waited until Dandy had wrestled the gloves on. He'd rigged a

trigger with one of Cocoa's elastic hair ties. Inside the toaster, he'd placed an old, outdated software CD.

Malcolm aimed. Dandy squatted, holding up his hands like a baseball catcher. "Stand up," Malcolm said. Dandy rose.

"Fire!" he yelled, launching the CD. It whizzed through the air, straight at Dandy.

Dandy ducked in the nick of time. The CD slammed into a tree a few feet behind him, shattering into several pieces.

"You didn't catch it!" Malcolm hollered.

Dandy looked a little pale. "Maybe I should've brought thicker gloves."

Malcolm loaded another CD. "Catch this one," he called.

Whoosh! Malcom's aim was off, and the CD went flying far beyond Dandy into some brush.

"That thing's as powerful as a rocket!" Dandy said. "Can I try it?"

"Sure," Malcolm told him. "But I only brought two CDs. We'll have to find that one first."

They headed into the heavy bushes, searching for it.

"It should be right here," Malcolm said. They went farther in.

"Maybe it went under one of those rocks," Dandy said, pointing to a group of large boulders.

They searched.

Then Malcolm saw it poking up, half under a boulder. When he reached for it, it slipped down under the rock.

"Hey! Where'd it go?" Dandy asked.

Malcolm reached his hand under. "Dandy, there's an opening here."

They moved some smaller rocks out of the way. Malcolm stuck his head in. "I should've brought a flashlight," he said.

Both boys lay flat, trying to see inside.

"You think it's a tunnel?" Dandy asked.

"No," Malcolm said. "I think it's a small cave. We've got to find a way in."

Dandy now had his face placed fully into the opening. "I don't know if I want to go in. It's kinda stinky."

Malcolm sniffed, then looked over at Dandy. "Yeah, it smells like a skunk!"

What's Inside?

"It could be that skunk from last night," Dandy said, hurrying behind Malcolm.

Malcolm was running now, heading back to camp. "It could be," he said. "But probably not."

"You really think it's Wild Willy?"

"I think it's his hideout. We've got to find something to dig with and get back there."

Malcolm rummaged through all the things their dads had brought—insect repellent, binoculars, and flashlights. Check!

They'd definitely needed flashlights. Malcolm switched them on to test them. Perfect. He threw one over to Dandy, then kept looking.

He found the food supply—trail mix, beef jerky, and a can of beans. *Beans?* If there are beans, there'd have to be a way to stir them. That's when Malcolm found a couple of large, sturdy spoons.

"We'll have to use these," he told Dandy, handing him one.

Dandy held up the items in his hands. "A flashlight and a spoon?"

Malcolm nodded. "For seeing and for digging."

Dandy examined the spoon. "We're going to dig through rock with this?"

"Nope. Just the dirt around it."

Malcolm stood, eager to get going. "Wait . . ." He headed to their small tent and pulled out his pack. "We better take this just in case." The specter detector gleamed in the sunlight.

"Are we gonna zap him?" Dandy asked.

"Yeah. But first, let's make sure it's him," Malcolm said.

The boys ran back to the clearing without stopping once. Not even when Dandy's shoelace came untied.

Malcolm clicked on the flashlight. "It smells worse than ever," he said.

Dandy scooched down next to him, trying to peer in with his flashlight too. "It looks pretty big."

Malcolm agreed. "Can you see anything?"

"Not much, but it looks like a cave all right."

"I just need to poke my head in some more. Let's dig."

They tried using the spoons to dig away the dirt and weeds. They made some progress, even though they mostly just managed to bend the spoons.

"Okay, let's try something else," Malcolm said. "You hold onto my feet while I squeeze my head and arms inside. We've got to be careful though. I wouldn't want to fall in."

"Okay," Dandy said, putting down his twisted spoon.

Malcolm shoved away some more of the dirt, hearing it splash inside the cave.

"I think there's water down there." He powered up his specter detector. Holding it in his left hand and the flashlight in his right, he squeezed in up to his chest.

"You see anything?" Dandy asked.

"Not yet, but I should've brought a clothespin for my nose." The smell was

overwhelming. Malcolm gagged a few times, then he tried holding his breath.

Using the flashlight, Malcolm scanned the cave. He saw a pile of twigs that looked like an animal's nest. *A skunk's?* A large bug skittered across the far wall. *Was that a scorpion?* Malcolm suddenly felt itchy.

"What do you see?" Dandy asked again, gripping Malcolm's ankles.

"Not much," Malcolm said. But as he said it, the flashlight's beam hit the large puddle of water standing at the bottom of the cave. Reflected in the water was the face of a man staring angrily up at Malcolm.

For the Birds

"Aaaaaah!" Malcolm tried pulling out of the opening, bumping his head on the rock.

Dandy tugged on his ankles, trying to yank him out faster. "What? What?"

"I saw him," Malcolm said, feeling shaky.

"You saw Wild Willy? What was he doing?"

"I only saw his face," Malcolm said.

Dandy stood there, holding Malcolm's ankles like he was gripping a wheelbarrow. "Oooooh, that's creepy. How'd you see his face?"

Malcolm shivered. "It was in a small pool of water."

Dandy dropped Malcolm's feet to the ground. "Are you sure it wasn't your own reflection?"

Malcolm rolled over and scooted away from the cave opening. "Do I have small, beady eyes?"

Dandy shook his head.

"Do I have a nose like a cauliflower?"

Dandy shook his head a little harder.

"Do I have a black cowboy hat on?"

Dandy looked, then shook his head.

"Trust me, that wasn't my reflection."

"So what do we do now?" Dandy wondered.

"We go get the ghost zapper," Malcolm answered.

When they got back to camp their dads were there. They were laughing as they untangled their fishing poles. "You almost had him," Mr. Dee said. "I swear that thing was four feet long!"

"Hey, guys," Malcolm's dad said as they walked up. "How was the Frisbee throwing?"

"Great!" Malcolm answered.

"After we rest up, we'll go on a hike. How about it?"

"Uh . . . sounds good, Dad, but we have some things to do first."

"What's that?" Malcolm's dad asked.

Malcolm glanced at Dandy, hoping for some help. Dandy gave a slight shrug. "Well . . . eh . . . Dandy and I are going bird-watching." He knew it sounded dumb as soon as he said it.

"Bird-watching?" Mr. Dee said, stepping forward. "That's great! Dandy knows how to imitate several birds."

Dandy fidgeted. "I haven't done that in a while, Dad."

"Come on," Mr. Dee egged. "Do a whip-poor-will for us."

"We're ready to head out," Malcolm said, trying to rescue his friend. But the words were barely out of his mouth when Dandy began to whistle. He sounded just like a bird! *Whip-poor-will! Whip-poor-will!*

"Very good!" Malcolm's dad said.

Malcolm gave Dandy a surprised look.

"I didn't know you could do that."

"You didn't know I could do this either." This time a sound came up from deep in his throat. *Coo-ooo! Coo-ooo!*

"Sounds just like a dove, doesn't it?" Mr. Dee said.

Malcolm's dad agreed. "You're amazing."

"And listen to this," Dandy said. He puckered his lips, but Malcolm grabbed him by his shirt and pulled. "Time to go," Malcolm said.

"Hey!" Instead of making a lovely birdcall, Dandy sputtered as Malcolm yanked him forward.

"All right, go look for birds," Mr. Dee said, shooing them with his hands.

Malcolm ducked into their tent and gathered a backpack full of items. Then

he found the first aid kit and pulled out some cotton balls. "Let's go," he told Dandy. They hurried back to the cave.

"Okay," Malcolm said. "We have to find a way in. I can't do this alone."

"Do what?" Dandy asked.

"I can't squeeze into the small opening while holding the flashlight, the specter detector, and the ghost zapper. I don't have enough hands."

Dandy scrunched up his face, thinking hard. "Maybe you could hold the flashlight in your mouth."

"Okay, not only would that be awkward, but I'd look pretty stupid too."

Malcolm searched the opening again. They'd made some progress with the spoons, but it was still too small. There had to be a way to make it bigger.

"Help me," he told Dandy. Malcolm sat on the ground to the side of the opening. Both of his feet were braced against one of the rocks next to the hole. Dandy did the same thing.

"Now push!" Malcolm said. They both strained, pushing against the rock as hard as they could. It moved about an inch.

They huffed and puffed, pushing with all their might. Another inch.

"Almost," Malcolm said.

With one more giant effort, the rock nudged a little more. The surrounding rocks gave way, opening an entrance on the side. The opening was big enough for both Malcolm and Dandy to squeeze through.

"Yes!" Malcolm said, his legs wobbly from all the pushing. The skunky smell grew stronger. "Ew!" He retrieved the

cotton balls and stuffed two up his nose. He handed a couple to Dandy. "Here."

Dandy, with cotton balls up his nose, peeked into the dark entrance. "Are we really going in?"

"Nope," Malcolm said.

Dandy looked relieved. "Good. Because it seems sort of dangerous."

"I'm going in," Malcolm said. He pulled a battery-powered lantern from his backpack.

"But I thought you didn't have enough hands," Dandy reminded him.

"That was when I had to squeeze in," Malcolm said. Next he pulled out some rope and tied it to his waist. "Tie the end of this to that huge rock."

Dandy wound the rope around the rock and triple-knotted it. "This still seems dangerous, even without a ghost inside."

"I won't be long," Malcolm said. He turned on the specter detector and tucked it into the waist of his jeans. Then, holding the ghost zapper in one hand and the flashlight in his mouth, he gripped the rope and lowered himself in.

The Challenge

The truth was, the drop down into the cave was only about four feet. When Dandy stuck the lantern in to look around, he hit Malcolm in the head.

"Ouch!"

"Oops!" Dandy said. "I thought the cave was a lot deeper."

Malcolm rubbed his head. "I wouldn't have come in if it had been deeper." He braved a step forward, trying to avoid the

large puddle. The cave was just one large room made of rock.

"How long do you think it's been hidden?" Dandy asked.

Malcolm shrugged. "I think those rocks were placed there on purpose. Just to keep people out."

"Maybe there's still gold hidden in there." Dandy stretched the lantern farther in, trying to see.

"I don't see anything that wasn't left here by an animal," Malcolm informed him. He remembered the scorpion and carefully moved away from the cave wall. "Besides, someone would've found it by now."

Malcolm did a full turn, then shone his flashlight down into the water. The only reflection he saw was his own. He took a few more steps in.

"You think Wild Willy is in there?" Dandy asked.

"It sure smells like it," Malcolm answered. "These cotton balls aren't working. We should've soaked them in my dad's aftershave first."

Suddenly a large, lumpy shadow appeared on the wall. "You don't like the way I smell?" a gruff voice said.

Malcolm whipped around. Right next to him stood the ghost of Wild Willy Wallace. His big, black mustache twitched. Then he cocked his hat and grinned.

"Zap him!" Dandy yelled, his shaky hand causing the lantern light to seesaw.

Wild Willy looked down at the zapper. A moment of panic crossed his hardened face. Then he turned his back. Glancing over his shoulder, he said, "You gonna zap me, boy? It's not right to go after a man with his back turned. That's just plain cowardly. You a coward?"

Malcolm wanted to say yes and zap the ghost, but he didn't want Dandy to think he was chicken. "I'm no coward," he told Wild Willy.

"Then let's do this proper," the old outlaw said. "Meet me at high noon. In the clearing."

"High noon? Won't someone see us?" Malcolm asked.

"That ain't my problem, boy." And with that, Wild Willy disappeared. His smell went with him.

Malcolm grabbed the rope and pulled himself out.

"What are you going to do?" Dandy asked.

"I'm meeting Wild Willy for a showdown at high noon."

"When's that?"

Malcolm looked at his watch. "In about fifteen minutes."

The Showdown

Malcolm and Dandy headed over to the clearing. There was no one around. The camping area seemed deserted, and they hadn't seen any hikers today. Malcolm was certain that had they been there during the summer it would be different. How lucky.

"So what's the plan?" Dandy asked, gripping the backpack.

Malcolm shrugged. "I'm not sure. I

guess I'll do just like Clint Eastwood in those old Westerns my dad loves."

"Can you make a face like Eastwood?"

"Why would I do that?" Malcolm asked.

"So you can show him who's boss. Like this." Dandy squinted his eyes and curled his lip.

"That doesn't look threatening," Malcolm said. "It looks like you have to use the bathroom."

"I do," Dandy said. "But that wasn't the face I was trying to make."

They waited. Malcolm checked his watch a gazillion times. The sun had risen higher in the sky. Because it was October, it wasn't directly overhead. At noon, it hid behind a large gray cloud.

They boys looked around as the seconds ticked by.

"Maybe he chickened out," Dandy said.

But they suddenly smelled skunk. Wild Willy appeared, standing in the spot near the heavy brush. "I ain't no chicken," he said. He took a couple of bowlegged steps forward, his hand hovering over his holster. "You ready to do this, boy?" he asked.

"Not really," Malcolm said, being honest. "I'm not sure I know the rules."

"Rules?" he said, letting out a wicked laugh. "I'll give you some rules." He swiped his hand across his brushy mustache. "First, we get rid of your pesky little friend here. I don't have no gripe with him." He pointed at Dandy.

"Nope," Malcolm said. "He stays with me."

Wild Willy grinned, showing a mouth full of rotten teeth. "I say he goes." And

with that, Wild Willy flung his arm like he was throwing something. A huge prickly tumbleweed appeared and came bouncing toward them.

Dandy turned to run, but the tumbleweed swallowed him up. He rolled off, yelling, "Malcolm! Get me out of here!"

"That should take care of him," Wild Willy said.

Malcolm wasn't sure what to do. Should he go after his friend or stay and finish the showdown?

"Well, boy," Wild Willy went on. "You ready for the next rule?"

Malcolm nodded, his mouth too dry to speak.

"I count to three. On three we draw."

"Wait!" Malcolm said, holding up his

hand. "We draw *when* you say three or *after* you say three?"

Wild Willy looked a tad annoyed. "We draw when I say 'draw'."

Malcolm was truly confused. He wanted to get this right. Maybe he should

just draw his ghost zapper before three and be done. Maybe he should just do that now. But what if Wild Willy saw him cheat and reached first?

"I know what you're thinking, boy," the outlaw said. "Don't go reaching too soon."

Rats! So much for that plan.

Wild Willy rubbed his stubbly chin. "Time's a wasting. You ready?"

"I'm ready," Malcolm said. He tried to sound menacing, but his voice came out a little too squeaky.

Wild Willy popped his knuckles, then wiggled his fingers over his holster again. "One . . ."

Malcolm's heart beat like a drum. Somewhere in the distance he heard a crow cawing.

"Two . . ."

Malcolm squinted his eyes and curled his lips. He hoped he looked like Clint Eastwood and not someone who had to go to the bathroom. More crows were cawing in the trees.

"Hear that?" Wild Willy said. "Those crows are singing a sad song for you."

"Maybe it's for you," Malcolm said. Even more crows joined in.

"Three . . . draw!"

Malcolm went for the ghost zapper. At that moment a flock of slick black crows swooped out of the trees, causing Wild Willy to flinch.

Malcolm drew first and unloaded the ghost zapper on him. Wild Willy melted into an oozy puddle with just his hat floating on top. Then with a *ping!* the hat popped like a bubble and disappeared.

Dandy's Secret

"**Y**ou did it!" Dandy said, rushing into the clearing.

"How'd you get out of that tumbleweed?" Malcolm asked.

Dandy held up the toaster and the CD. "I blasted my way out with the Super Toss."

"Good thinking."

Dandy stared down at the puddle, which was quickly soaking into the

ground. "Guess we won't be smelling him anymore."

"Guess not," Malcolm said. He looked at the ghost zapper. "I don't think I'm a very quick draw though. If it hadn't been for those crows, Wild Willy would've won."

Dandy grinned. "Don't give those crows all the credit." He leaned his head back and went, "Caw! Caw! Caw!"

"You called those crows?" Malcolm asked.

"Yep," Dandy said.

"How come you never told me you could do that?"

Dandy shrugged. "You never asked."

As they approached the camp, the dads were busy building a campfire. "Just in time!" Malcolm's dad called out. "We're about to rustle up some hot lunch."

"Good," Dandy said, sitting down at a picnic table. "I'm starving."

Mr. Dee pulled out a can of beans. "Did you see any interesting birds?" he asked, twisting the can opener.

Malcolm smiled at Dandy. Dandy grinned back. "We saw a whole flock of crows," Malcolm said.

"Crows!" Mr. Dee said. "No wattlebirds? Magpies? Scissortail?"

Malcolm shook his head. "We didn't see any of those." He sat down too, feeling both hungry and tired.

"Well," Malcolm's dad said, "maybe

we'll spot some interesting ones when we go hiking after lunch."

"Yeah," Malcolm agreed. "Maybe Dandy can call some down for us."

Dandy puckered his lips, whistling like a songbird.

Mr. Dee rubbed his palms together. "It won't be long now. I just need to stir up these beans . . . hey! What happened to our spoons?"

"Uh-oh." Malcolm looked over at Dandy and winked.

FIVE MORE WAYS TO DETECT A GHOST, SPIRIT, OR POLTERGEIST

From Ghost Detectors Malcolm and Dandy

21. Ghost stories are often based on true stories! Campfires and sleepovers are the best times tell ghost stories.

22. Legendary outlaws may seem exciting, but don't search for them unless you are armed with an Ecto-Handheld-Automatic-Heat-Sensitive-Laser-Enhanced Ghost Zapper.

23. If a legend includes a certain smell, its ghost may have the same scent. Use your nose wisely (but watch out for skunks)!

24. If a person turns on his gang in real life, he probably won't be a friendly spirit! Watch out for those ghosts.

25. Caves, hollowed-out trees, and ponds are good hiding places for spirits. Check them carefully!